This Little Tiger book belongs to:

_____

_____

_____

For Dylan, with all my love x
~ T C

For Karyn Anderton
~ T M

LITTLE TIGER PRESS LTD,
an imprint of the Little Tiger Group
1 Coda Studios, 189 Munster Road,
London SW6 6AW
www.littletiger.co.uk

First published in Great Britain 2011
This edition published 2017

Oh Dylan!

by Tracey Corderoy • Illustrated by Tina Macnaughton

LITTLE TIGER

LONDON

One breezy day, four little ducklings were making a daisy chain.

"Pick and thread!" chanted Polly, Molly and Holly.

"Look at me!" chuckled Dylan, all tied up in a big flowery knot!

"Now," said Mother Duck, "we're off to the pond for your very first swim. Hold on to the daisy chain and then you won't get lost."

"It's a choo-choo chain!" cried Dylan. "Choo-choo!"

Polly, Molly, Holly and Dylan skipped along behind
Mother Duck, singing a springtime song . . .

"Four little ducklings all in a row,
Skipping across the bridge we go!
Wiggle our tails – we're on our way
Down to the pond to splash and play!"

Suddenly, the ducklings spotted a beautiful,
blue feather.

"So pretty!" gasped Polly, Molly and Holly.

"Come back!" cried Dylan as the feather
blew away.

Then he had a *wonderful* idea . . .

On the other side of the bridge,
some baby lambs were playing
catch-the-petals.

"*We* want to play too!" said Polly.

"All right," smiled Mother Duck. She counted
her ducklings as they hopped off the bridge.
"Polly, Molly, Holly and . . .

"OH MY!" she gasped.
"Where's Dylan?"

All in a fluster
and a flap, everyone
searched for Dylan.

Suddenly, Molly spotted him stuck up a tree!
"Surprise!" cried Dylan. "I got the pretty
feather for you!"

"Oh, *Dylan*," said Mother Duck. "You *are* a sweetie!
But what did I say about not getting lost?
Now hold on to the choo-choo chain."
"And don't let go!" quacked Polly.

On they went into the woods, singing their song . . .

"Four little ducklings all in a row,
Counting the flowers as we go!
Flutter our wings — we're on our way
Down to the pond to dive and play!"

"Mmmm, *lovely*!" cried the sisters, sniffing the flowers.
"A-ccchhhoooo!" sneezed Dylan.
Then he had a *wonderful* idea . . .

At the top of a hill, some baby hedgehogs were playing roly-poly!

"*We* want to roll too!" said Polly.

"All right," smiled Mother Duck. She counted her ducklings as they tumbled down the hill. "Polly, Molly, Holly and . . .

"WAIT!" she flapped. "Where's Dylan?"

With wings a-flutter and
feathers flying, everyone
searched for Dylan.
Then suddenly a whirlwind of
fluff came spinning towards them . . .

"Surprise!" cried Dylan. "I picked some pretty flowers for you!"

"Oh, *Dylan,*" said Mother Duck. "You *are* kind! But you forgot what I told you *again* . . ."

"Don't let go of the daisy chain!" yelled his sisters.

On they waddled, under a hedge and *at last* they saw . . .

. . . the pond!
"*Phew!*" gasped Mother Duck.
"All safely here!"

Polly, Molly and Holly dipped their
toes into the water.
"But it's *c-c-cold*!" they shivered.
"We don't like it!"

Then suddenly,

splash!

Dylan was in . . .

. . . and – *wow* – this was *fun*!

"Look!" cried Dylan. "Look at me!"
He splished and splashed and swam
and swam until, all too soon, it was
time to go.

On the way home, Dylan felt so very clever! He
could *swim* and Mother Duck had said he was great!
He yawned as a big, silver moon lit the sky.
Then he and his sisters sang one final song . . .

"Four sleepy ducklings all in a row,
Waddling back for supper we go.
Tiny stars begin to peep,
Soon we'll all be fast asleep . . ."

When they got home, Mother Duck
baked something warm and tasty.
Then she counted her ducklings
around the table.

"Polly, Molly, Holly and . . .
Oh *dear*," she sighed. "Not
again! *Where's Dylan?*"

Polly wriggled, Molly giggled, but Holly
whispered in Mother Duck's ear. They peeped
around the door . . .

. . . and there, curled up in his
choo-choo chain, was *Dylan*.
    "Nighty-night," giggled Polly,
Molly and Holly as he gave
a tiny snore.
    "Sleep tight," whispered Mother Duck.
"Sweet dreams!"